This book belongs to

....

GW00788082

ISBN 978-1-84135-836-9

Text adapted from original stories by Karen King

Copyright © Award Publications Limited

This collection first published 2017

Published by Award Publications Limited,
The Old Riding School, Welbeck,
Worksop, S80 3LR

www.awardpublications.co.uk

17 1

Printed in China

Tales of
Magical
Horses

Stories by Karen King

Illustrated by Angela Hicks

Award Publications Limited

Unicorn Magic

Ivory was the youngest and smallest of all the unicorns who lived in the meadow by the Enchanted Forest. And that meant she couldn't always join in with the others.

"Can I go?" she asked, when they went to gather fruit.

"No, you're too little," her mother said. "You might get caught in the brambles."

"Can I go?" she asked, when
the other young unicorns went off to explore the forest.

"No, Ivory," her father said. "You're not old enough yet,
and you might get lost."

So Ivory had to stay at home.

It was the same when she wanted to play with her bigger unicorn friends.
   "You'll be too slow to keep up," they said.
   Ivory was fed up with being told that she was too little to do anything.

"I'm going to go to the forest all by myself!" she thought.

But she knew she wasn't supposed to go off on her own. "I'll only go a little way," she told herself.

Ivory was so excited as she wandered into the forest to explore.

As she followed the trail she began to feel hungry, so she trotted over to a berry bush. Taking care to avoid the thorns, she nibbled at a few berries among the brambles.

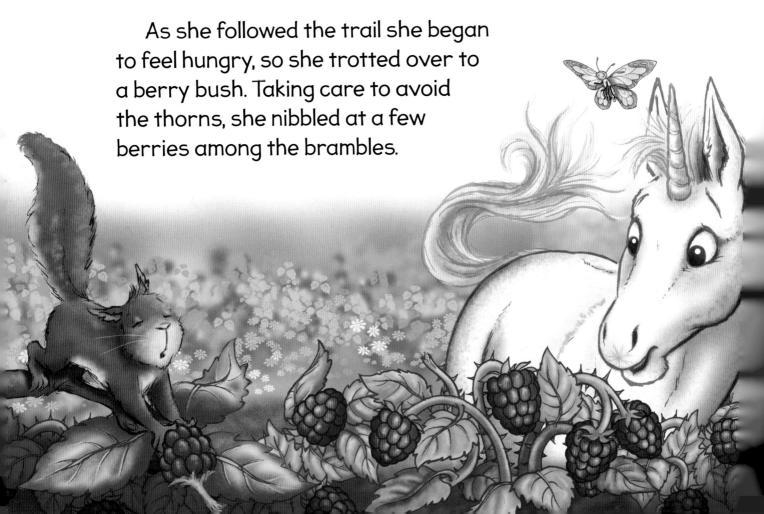

"Even little unicorns
can pick berries,"
Ivory thought, feeling
proud of herself. Then
she needed a drink.

She closed her eyes and
sniffed. Her nose tingled,
which meant there must be
water nearby. Following her
nose, she soon came to
a stream.

"Even little unicorns can find water," she thought as she lapped at the stream.

Feeling tired, Ivory lay down to rest and soon fell asleep. When she finally woke up it was getting late.

"Oh, I'd better hurry home!" she thought. "Everyone will wonder where I am."

But as Ivory trotted back along the path, she almost tripped over a wood nymph who was sitting at the foot of a tree, sobbing.

"What's the matter?" Ivory asked.

The startled nymph looked up in surprise. "Oh my! A unicorn! I've found one!" she cried.

"What do you mean?" asked Ivory, puzzled.

"My mother is very ill," the nymph explained. "The healer said that only a hair from a unicorn can make her better." She gulped back a sob. "Please could I take a hair from your tail?"

"Of course," agreed Ivory. "Just pull one out."

The nymph quickly pulled a long golden hair from Ivory's tail.

Then she placed it carefully in a locket she wore around her neck.

"Thank you so much! Now I must hurry back."

"I'll take you home," offered Ivory. "It will be much quicker!"

Gratefully, the little nymph climbed onto Ivory's back. "I'm afraid it's quite a long way," she said.

"Then I'll have to gallop," said Ivory. "Hold tight!"

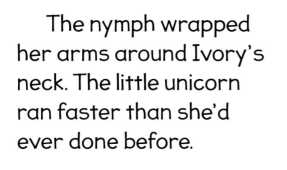

The nymph wrapped her arms around Ivory's neck. The little unicorn ran faster than she'd ever done before.

At first, Ivory seemed to fly through the forest, leaping over fallen logs and dodging between bramble bushes.

She was determined to get the nymph home in time to save her mother.

But it was a long way
for a young unicorn, and
Ivory began to tire.

"I must keep going," she
told herself. "I might be little,
but I'm sure I can do it!"

20

On and on she galloped.

When they came to a small wooden bridge the nymph cried, "We're almost there!"

Ivory spotted a strange little house in a tree trunk. "That's my home," said the nymph. "I hope we're not too late."

The nymph hurried into the house.

As the moon rose, Ivory lay down to wait.
She was so weary that she soon fell asleep again.

At last the cottage door opened and
Ivory jumped up.
"The magic worked!" said the nymph,
smiling happily. "My mother is feeling
better already! Thank you!"

"You're welcome," said Ivory. "Even little unicorns are magical!" she thought.

Ivory looked up at the moon. "I must go home now," she said. "I hope I see you again."

"Me too," said the nymph as she waved goodbye.

The forest
was now very
dark and there
were shadows
everywhere.
Ivory felt scared.
    What if she
couldn't find her
way home?

Suddenly a huge shadow loomed
across the path ahead.

"There you are!"
Ivory recognised the voice at once.
"Father? What are you doing here?"
Ivory neighed happily.
She was so pleased
to see him.

25

"I was looking for you," he replied. "We were very worried when you disappeared."

"I'm sorry," said Ivory. "I was fed up with everyone telling me I was too little to do anything."

Ivory told him all about how she helped the nymph.
"You've been very brave, but you must always tell
someone where you are going," said her father.
And though she was indeed a brave little unicorn,
Ivory never went running off by herself again!

The Little
Fairy Horse

Cobweb was a magical fairy horse who lived in Fairy Glen.

Today was a very special day. The Fairy Queen was going to announce which horses would pull her golden coach to the fairies' Midsummer Ball.

"The Fairy Queen won't pick you, Cobweb," said Sapphire. "You haven't had any practice. You'd just all get tangled up."

"Besides, only the most elegant fairy horses can pull the coach," added Dazzle. She looked pointedly at Cobweb's messy tail and mane.

Cobweb blushed as the other fairy horses teased her. It was her dream to pull the golden coach.

"I'll show you all," she declared. "I'll be chosen, just you wait and see!"

Ignoring their laughter, she fluttered home.

"Oh, Cobweb!" her mother sighed, as Cobweb landed with a splash right in a muddy puddle. "You could try to land a little more gently. It is much more graceful, and you'd be able to see where you're going too!"

"I'm sorry," said Cobweb. "I do try."

"I know you do," said her mother gently. "But if you want the Fairy Queen to chose you, you will have to try a bit harder."

She looked down at Cobweb's muddy hooves. "You'll need to make sure that you're well-groomed too."

Cobweb glanced down at her hooves, feeling sheepish.

"Go and clean yourself up," her mother suggested. "And I'll ask my fairy friends to see if they can help you get ready for the Choosing."

Cobweb went to the stream to wash off the mud. Two fairies brushed her mane and polished her wings. Then they wove colourful ribbons and flowers into her tail.

"Perfect!" smiled her mother. "Now, you'd better go or you'll be late. And whatever you do, don't get dirty."

"I won't!" Cobweb promised.
"And trot, don't gallop!" her
mother called after her.

But she hadn't gone very
far when she came across a
big muddy puddle in the
middle of the path.

Remembering her
mother's warning, she
stepped around it carefully.

"Help!" croaked a strange voice. "Please stop! Don't leave me here!" Cobweb looked down and saw a toad.

"I've hurt my leg," said the toad. "Would you mind helping me out of this mud and taking me to the stream?" Cobweb didn't want to be late for the Choosing. And the toad was very muddy. She hesitated.

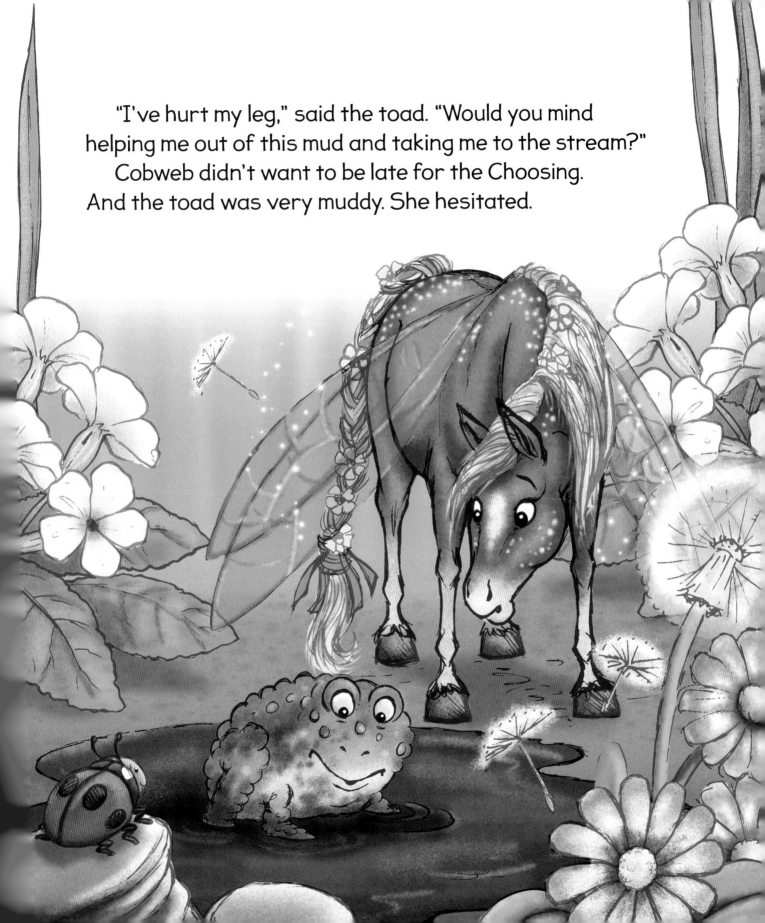

"I'm sorry, I'm in such a rush," Cobweb explained. "I'm on my way to the palace. The Fairy Queen is choosing the horses to pull her golden coach today."

"Oh," sighed the toad. "I understand. You should go. Hopefully someone else will help."

But Cobweb felt bad.
"I will help you," she said.
Using her newly plaited
tail, she pulled the toad
out of the mud.

"Hold tight!"
she said, and off
they flew to the
stream.

As soon as they landed, the toad thanked her, slipped off her back and dived into the water.

Cobweb looked at her muddy tail and sighed. "I'll never be chosen to pull the queen's golden coach now," she thought sadly.

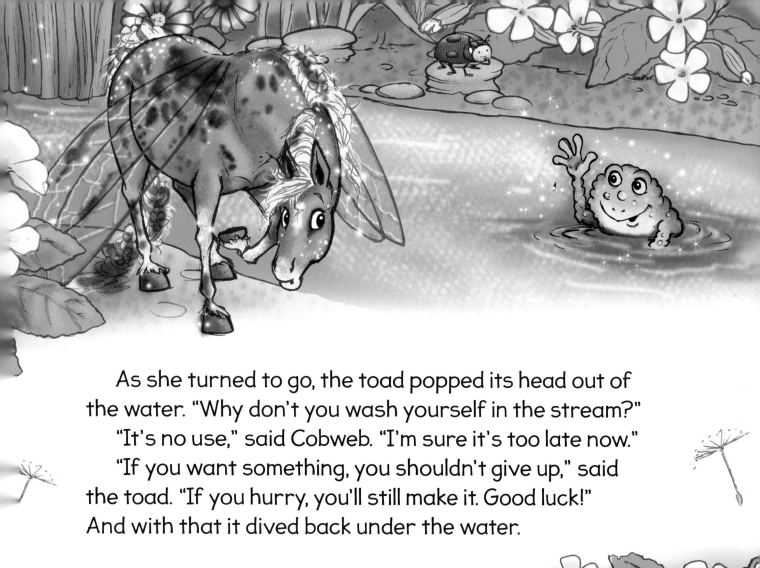

As she turned to go, the toad popped its head out of the water. "Why don't you wash yourself in the stream?"

"It's no use," said Cobweb. "I'm sure it's too late now."

"If you want something, you shouldn't give up," said the toad. "If you hurry, you'll still make it. Good luck!" And with that it dived back under the water.

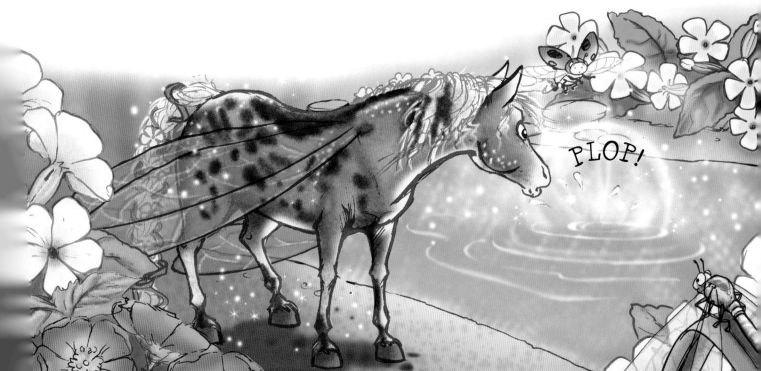

PLOP!

Cobweb plunged into the stream to wash off the mud, but all her pretty flowers and ribbons came loose and floated away.

She looked a little less elegant now, but she set off for the palace anyway, determined to try her best.

By the time she arrived, the first four horses had already been chosen.

"Oh, Cobweb. You'll never be picked looking like that," Sapphire chuckled.

Even though she felt upset, Cobweb knew Sapphire was right.

But then Cobweb heard someone call her name. Could it be? Cobweb looked back. "Cobweb!" The Fairy Queen herself was calling her.

"The muddy toad that you helped was me in disguise," the queen explained. "I wanted to see which fairy horse had a heart of gold. You were the only one who stopped to help me. So you deserve to pull my golden coach."

Cobweb was speechless.

With her shimmering wand, the Fairy Queen turned Cobweb's mane and tail into spun gold, and sprinkled glittering fairy dust over her wings. The other fairy horses gasped in surprise.

"There! Now you shall lead my team of horses," said the Fairy Queen.

47

It was a magical Midsummer Ball
that Cobweb would never forget.

Everyone cheered for the
Fairy Queen when they saw the
glorious golden coach travelling
across the sky.

But it was Cobweb, with her shimmering wings, who
stole the show. She was the prettiest, most graceful –
and, of course, kind-hearted – fairy horse that anyone
had ever seen.

Sparkle
the Sea Horse

Sparkle the sea horse lived on a beautiful coral reef. Although she had many friends, she was the only sea horse.

"If only there was someone else like me," she sighed, watching the other fish playing together. "Then we could be best friends."

"Well, why don't you go and look for one?" said Snap, the wise old lobster. "You can't be the only sea horse."

"What, leave the reef?" gasped Sparkle. She'd never swum away from her home before.

"It's the only way to find out," said Snap.

Swimming away from the reef was a scary idea,
but Sparkle really wanted to find a sea horse friend.
"Right, I will do it," she decided.
And before she could change her mind, she set
off into the unknown ocean beyond the reef.

On and on she swam, past towering rock pillars and out into the deep ocean. The further she went, the bigger and more scary-looking the fish became.

"Oh dear," Sparkle thought. "This doesn't feel safe. Maybe it's not such a good idea."

Just then a huge octopus came out of its cave. Sparkle plucked up the courage and asked him if he had seen any other sea horses like her.

"No, I'm sorry," replied the octopus kindly. "You're the first I've ever met."

"Perhaps I really am the only sea horse in
the whole wide ocean," Sparkle thought sadly.
   She was about to give up when she spotted a little
clown fish searching frantically among the seaweed.

"Hello!" said Sparkle.

The clown fish looked up in surprise. "Wow! Are you a sea horse?"

"Yes, but I think I'm the only one," Sparkle sighed. "Who are you?"

"My name is Coco. I'm a juggler," the clown fish said.

58

"I'm supposed to be performing at the Crab King's birthday party," Coco continued, "but I was in a rush and dropped my juggling balls – and now I can't find them anywhere!"

"I could help you look for them," offered Sparkle.

So together they started to search the seabed for Coco's juggling balls.

Suddenly Sparkle spotted a glint of something shiny. She swam over and swished the sand away from it with her tail. It was a glittering red ball.

"I've found one!" she cried.

"And here's another!" said Coco.

They popped the balls into Coco's bag.
"The last one can't be far away," Sparkle said.
They searched again, but to no avail. "I must go or I'll be terribly late," said Coco. "Thank you for your help!"
"Good luck!" Sparkle waved as Coco swam off.

By now Sparkle was feeling
hungry, so she nibbled at
some seaweed. As she ate,
something red caught her eye
among the pebbles.

"Coco! I've found it!"
Sparkle called excitedly.

Luckily, Coco hadn't swum very far.

"You've saved my show!" she smiled, as Sparkle gave her the ball. "How can I thank you?"

"Well," Sparkle said. "I'm looking for other sea horses, but so far I haven't been able to find any."

"You should come to the party with me!" Coco said excitedly. "I'm sure the Crab King will know if there are any around here!"

"Could I really?" Sparkle beamed. "That would be wonderful, thank you!"

64

Coco led Sparkle to the Crab King's palace, which was beautifully decorated with seaweed garlands for the party. Lots of sea creatures were already there, dancing and having fun. In the middle of it all was the Crab King himself, sitting on the royal throne.

"The juggler has arrived, Your Majesty!" an angel fish announced. "She has brought a sea horse with her!"

"Why, this is marvellous news!" exclaimed the king.

As he spoke, a purple sea horse shyly peeped out from behind his throne.

66

"Well, Aqua," the king smiled, turning to the purple sea horse, "I can hardly believe I'm lucky enough to have two sea horses at my party!"

"I can't believe it either," whispered Aqua. "I was beginning to think I was the only one in the whole ocean."

"Me too!" laughed Sparkle.

Then it was then time for Coco's juggling act.
Everyone clapped and cheered as she juggled the balls
with great skill, performing trick after trick.
"Amazing!" Sparkle and Aqua chorused.

There were many more performances
too – a singing starfish, acrobatic flying fish
and a troupe of dancing shrimps.
      Sparkle and Aqua had a wonderful time
together. When the party finally ended, they
didn't want to say goodbye.

"Why don't you come home with me and meet my friends?" Sparkle suggested.

Aqua was delighted. "Oh, I'd love to!"

The deep ocean wasn't so scary now Sparkle had a friend beside her. They talked excitedly all the way, and soon reached the coral reef.

70

Snap the lobster was thrilled to see them. "So, you did find another sea horse!"

"Yes," said Sparkle happily. "I'm not the only one, after all!"

"And neither am I!" smiled Aqua.

Moonlight
and the Mermaid

Moonlight was a little winged horse. He and his friends loved to fly. They often played hide and seek among the fluffy white clouds, or dared each other to see who could fly the highest.

Sometimes at night-time they would fly among
the shooting stars before they went to bed.
But they never flew out across the vast blue
sea. They knew it was much too dangerous.

"You mustn't fly over the sea until you are much bigger," Moonlight's mother told him. "If your wings get tired, you'll fall into the sea, and we can't swim like other horses."

But Moonlight was fascinated by the ocean.

He would often stand on the shore and stare out across the water, wondering what lay beyond.

"One day I'm going to fly all the way across the ocean!" he said to himself.

One evening as Moonlight was playing near the cliffs, he heard a faint, faraway cry.

It sounded like someone was in trouble. He strained his ears to hear it more clearly. "Help! Oh, someone please help me!" wailed the voice. "I'm stranded!"

Moonlight spotted a young
mermaid, waving frantically
from a rock on the beach below.
He flew down towards her.

79

"Oh, thank you!" said the mermaid.

"What's wrong?" asked Moonlight. "And what are you doing here out of the water?"

The mermaid explained how she had swum over to the rock earlier that day to sit in the sun and comb her hair.

"Then I fell asleep," she said, "and the tide went out."
"I can take you down to the sea," Moonlight offered.
The mermaid shook her head. "I've been out of the
sea so long my tail is too stiff. I'll need to rub in some
special coral lotion to soften it before I can swim again."

81

"I could get the lotion for you!" offered Moonlight.
"But it's at home." The mermaid started to sob. "And if
I don't get it soon I might never be able to swim again!"
Moonlight felt very sorry for her. "Don't cry. I'll take
you home," he said.
"Where do you live?"

"It's far from here," said the mermaid sadly. "I live in the middle of the sea, near Coral Island."

Moonlight looked out over the waves. In the middle of the sea! Did he dare fly so far from land? If he didn't, the poor mermaid might be stranded forever.

"I will fly you there!" he said bravely.

Moonlight knelt down. "Hop on, and hold on tight."

The mermaid climbed carefully onto his back. "Oh, thank you!" she said.

With a deep breath Moonlight spread his wings and leapt into the night sky. As he flew over the silvery sea, he hoped his wings wouldn't get too tired.

"I am a strong, brave pegasus. I can do it!"
he told himself.

"This is so exciting!" cried the mermaid.
"I've never flown before!"

85

"Look, what a big ship!" gasped the mermaid as they passed a huge ocean liner. Moonlight swooped down to see it better.

He was so fast and bright, the ship's passengers thought he must be shooting star.

On and on they flew, past leaping dolphins, a big blue whale and shoals of flying fish, until at last an island came into sight.

"That's my home!" cried the mermaid.

"I did it!" thought Moonlight as he flew down to the lagoon.

As he landed, mermaids and mermen swam up to greet them.

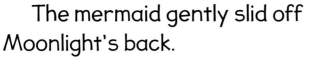

The mermaid gently slid off
Moonlight's back.

"Teela! Where have you been?"
asked her father.

"I got stranded on the shore," she
said. "But this kind young pegasus
saved me."

"Thank you for bringing her home,"
said Teela's mother, as she started to
rub coral lotion into Teela's tail.

"Yes, thank you!" said Teela. "Let me give you something for helping me." She plaited some seaweed into Moonlight's tail.

"This is magical sea kelp. Wherever you fly, its magic will ensure you always come home safely," she said.

"Thank you!" Moonlight gasped.

"Please come back and visit us again," Teela called as Moonlight set off for home. "I will!" he promised.

The other flying horses were anxiously waiting for him on the shore.

When he finally returned they were so relieved.

"Where have you been?" his mother asked. "I was afraid you had fallen into the sea."

"I'm sorry," he said. "I know I shouldn't have gone without telling you. I didn't mean to worry you, but someone needed my help."

He told everyone all about his wonderful adventure.

After that, Moonlight often visited Teela and her friends. And thanks to the mermaids' magic, he always returned home safely.